DOGGONE . . . THIRD GRADE!

DOGGONE . . . THIRD GRADE!

by COLLEEN O'SHAUGHNESSY McKENNA

illustrated by STEPHANIE ROTH

Holiday House / New York

Text copyright © 2002 by Colleen O'Shaughnessy McKenna
Illustrations copyright © 2002 by Stephanie Roth
All Rights Reserved
Printed in the United States of America
First Edition
www.holidayhouse.com

Library of Congress Cataloging-in-Publication Data
McKenna, Colleen O'Shaughnessy.
Doggone . . . third grade! / by Colleen O'Shaughnessy McKenna;
illustrated by Stephanie Roth—1st ed.
p. cm.
Summary: Third-grader Gordie is not only having problems with his
best friend, he also has to teach his not-so-smart dog some tricks
for the upcoming school talent show.
ISBN 0-8234-1696-8 (hardcover)
[1. Best friends—Fiction. 2. Dogs—Fiction. 3. Talent shows—Fiction.
4. Schools—Fiction. 5. Humorous stories.] I. Roth, Stephanie, ill. II. Title.

PZ7.M478675 Do 2002
[Fic]—dc21
2001039280

To my much-loved friend, Sally Alexander,
and the memory of her dog Ursula,
who guided her so well.
C. O. M.

To Matthew Baker,
amazing friend.
S. R.

Chapter

1

"I want to stay in third grade forever, Lamont," Gordie said to his best friend. "Even when I'm fifty."

"Me too," Lamont said. "We'll be old enough to drive to school then."

"We can be bus drivers!" Gordie said. "We'll give candy to all the kids on our bus!"

Lamont scrambled out of his seat. "Cool! We'll let dogs ride our bus."

"We'll make them bus patrol dogs!"

Lamont and Gordie slapped high five.

The first bell rang and Miss Tingle flashed the lights. That's what she did to make the kids in room 9 sit down and stop talking. Flashing lights was a lot nicer than yelling.

"I have some exciting news for room nine," Miss Tingle said.

"Yippee, pizza for lunch!" cried Gordie.

Miss Tingle laughed. "Better than pizza, Gordie. Our class is going to have a talent show."

A few kids clapped. Lucy stood up and waved her hand. "Oh, oh, Miss Tingle! I was in a talent show this summer at my uncle's bowling alley. I sang two songs and then I did cartwheels all the way down the alley."

Gordie frowned. Lucy was always bragging about something. He had to share a locker with her. He wanted to share with Lamont. Lamont never bragged.

"And, I can even draw pictures with my eyes closed." Lucy drew in a deep breath and sat down. She popped right back up again. "Plus, I can play the piano . . . sort of."

"I can play the piano with both hands," called out Mikey.

Miss Tingle smiled. "That's wonderful. I'm sure each child in room nine has a very interesting talent."

2

Lucy waved her hand. "I have the most talents, Miss Tingle. Maybe I should take *two* turns in the show."

Gordie poked Lamont in the arm. "Do you think she can make herself disappear?"

Lamont laughed. "Presto, no more Lucy!"

Miss Tingle frowned. "Boys, do you have something to say?"

Gordie sat up straighter. "No, Miss Tingle." Miss Tingle didn't like anyone to be mean. She said room 9 was one big happy family. But Gordie didn't feel like Lucy was a sister. Mostly he thought of her as a pain in the neck.

Miss Tingle smiled at Gordie. She never stayed mad. Not even when Joey Martin threw up in her trash can.

Lamont raised his hand. "My uncle has a talent."

"What is his talent?" asked Miss Tingle.

"He can make a jar of pickles disappear!"

"How does he make the pickles disappear?" Miss Tingle asked.

"He eats them!" Lamont said.

Everyone laughed. Miss Tingle shook her head and grinned.

"That's not a talent!" snapped Lucy. "It's called *eating*."

Lamont waved his hand. "And, my uncle Herbie knows how to swallow snakes."

Gordie shuddered. He'd met Uncle Herbie once. He was as big as a tree. His hands were the size of dinner plates.

"I bet you're lying." Lucy got out of her seat and stared at Lamont. "Nobody eats snakes, Lamont."

Lamont grinned. "What about candy gummy snakes?"

Miss Tingle clapped her hands. Gordie saw that she wasn't smiling so much anymore. "We only have a few days to put together the show, so let's start planning."

Lamont raised his hand again. "Miss Tingle, call on me."

Miss Tingle smiled at Lamont. "Is this a *real* talent, Lamont?"

Lamont nodded. "I can play the guitar. My brother taught me this summer."

Miss Tingle got out a piece of chalk. "Let's list room nine's talents."

More and more kids raised their hands. Miss Tingle's list got longer and longer. Miss Tingle's chalk got shorter and shorter.

Gordie looked at the list. He wanted his name on the board. But, he didn't know how to sing or dance. He didn't know how to play the piano. He couldn't draw very well. All his animals looked like cats. Even his cows looked like cats.

After ten minutes, Miss Tingle put down the chalk. "Have we heard from everyone?"

"You haven't heard from Gordie!" Lucy called out.

Gordie slumped deeper into his seat. Lucy sure had a big mouth. She had the biggest mouth in the whole school.

"Gordie, what are you going to do for the show?" Miss Tingle asked gently.

Gordie shrugged. "I don't know yet." He bit his lip. "I can ride a two-wheeler. With no hands."

"So can everyone in the whole wide world," said Lucy. "That doesn't count,

Gordie. Plus, there are too many desks in here. You'd ride into the fish tank."

"Ha, ha, very funny," mumbled Gordie. He stared at his desk while a few kids laughed. Lamont reached over and patted his arm.

"Would you like to do something else, Gordie?" asked Miss Tingle.

Gordie sat up straighter. "I know how to spell lots of words."

Lucy flipped her hair over her shoulders. "Boring!"

Miss Tingle snapped her fingers. "That's enough, Lucy."

Lucy pretended she was looking for something in her desk. Nobody liked to be yelled at by Miss Tingle. Lucy popped her head out of her desk. "Gordie can have one of my talents."

Miss Tingle smiled. "That's nice to share, Lucy. But I'm sure Gordie has his own talent."

"Yeah," said Gordie. But his voice wasn't very loud.

"He has lots of them," said Lamont. "Real good ones."

"Great," said Miss Tingle. "Can I write one down?"

Gordie had a great idea. "I know. I'll be the audience."

Everyone laughed. Miss Tingle smiled. "We're inviting Mr. Johnson's class to watch our show."

"What?" Gordie thumped his head down on his desk.

"Cool," said Lucy. "The big kids are coming."

"Is everything okay, Gordie?" asked Miss Tingle.

"No," Gordie mumbled. Two things were very wrong. First of all, he didn't have a talent. Second of all, his big brother, Doug, was in Mr. Johnson's room. Doug and all his friends would boo Gordie for not having a talent.

Gordie raised his hand to ask Miss Tingle if he could go lie down on the nurse's couch. Maybe he could catch some germs there. He was busy waving his hand when someone knocked on the door.

Chapter

2

Everyone turned and watched Miss Tingle open the door. The principal, Mr. Fratorolli, walked in. A tall boy with bright orange hair followed him.

"Good morning, Miss Tingle. Good morning, class," said Mr. Fratorolli. "I have a special surprise for you this morning."

"This must be Richard Jenkins," said Miss Tingle. She reached out her hand and Richard shook it. "Welcome to room nine, Richard."

"Richard prefers to be called Red," said Mr. Fratorolli. He handed Miss Tingle some papers and waved good-bye.

Gordie stared at Red. He wished he had a cool nickname. His brother called him

Shrimp, but Gordie didn't want other people calling him that, especially since he was the shortest kid in room 9. Red's hair was the nice orange color of a new basketball.

"I know you will enjoy meeting the children in this school," said Miss Tingle. "Why don't you sit in front of Lamont? Lamont, raise your hand."

Red nodded. He kept his eyes on the floor as he walked down the aisle. His cheeks were getting pink and he kept swallowing. Gordie decided to tell Red at lunch that kids were only staring because their school didn't get many new kids. They weren't staring because of his hair.

"Boy, you sure have bright hair," said Lucy.

"Lucy," snapped Miss Tingle.

Lucy looked surprised. "I'm not being rude. He has great hair, kind of like it's plugged into electricity. My aunt Loretta has red hair and that's why she gets to do commercials on TV. She sells salad dressing and mouthwash."

"That's enough, Lucy," said Miss Tingle.

Red smiled. "That's okay. I do commercials, too."

Gordie leaned closer. The new kid was on TV?

"You do commercials for television?" asked Miss Tingle.

Red looked up. "Well, not me, but my dog, Lawrence, does commercials. He sells dog food and flea shampoo."

"Cool!" cried Lucy. "Bring your dog to school and he can be in our talent show."

Lucy added, "He can have Gordie's turn in the show. He doesn't have a talent."

"Lucy—" began Miss Tingle.

"I do, too," said Gordie. "And *my* dog has a talent, too."

Lamont stared at Gordie. "Scratch knows tricks?"

"Yeah," said Gordie. He felt bad lying to his best friend, but the whole class was looking at him. Scratch didn't even know how to roll over.

"Oh, yeah?" said Lucy. "Well, I saw your dog when I went trick-or-treating and he looked pretty dumb to me. In fact, he hid

under your porch when a ghost came up and said, 'Trick or treat.'"

"Sit down, Lucy," said Miss Tingle. "Gordie will decide on his talent when he is ready." She checked her watch. "We had better take out our spellers or we'll be late for lunch."

Lamont raised his hand. "Miss Tingle?"

"Yes, Lamont?"

Gordie sat up straight and smiled.

Lamont was probably going to tell Miss Tingle to throw Lucy out of third grade for having such a big mouth.

But Lamont said, "Red can eat lunch with me. I can show him around the school so he won't get lost."

"How nice of you, Lamont," said Miss Tingle.

Gordie nodded. He'd help show Red around, too. He could take him upstairs and show him all the fifth-graders.

The room got noisy as desk tops went up and spelling books were slapped on the desks. Mikey and Lucy raced up to sharpen their pencils. Lucy always had to be first in line, even for pencil-sharpening.

"Lamont," whispered Gordie.

But Lamont was already out of his seat, asking Miss Tingle for a speller for Red. Miss Tingle got one from the cupboard and smiled at him.

Gordie tried to grab Lamont's arm as he raced past. But then he was busy giving Red his special pencil, the one he'd gotten at Disney World.

"Thanks," said Red. "I'll give it back tomorrow."

Lamont loved that pencil so much, Gordie had never even asked to borrow it. Or touch it.

"That's okay," said Lamont. "You can just keep it."

Gordie's mouth fell open, then clamped together hard as Lamont and Red smiled and gave each other high fives.

Gordie opened his speller and tried not to watch Lamont and Red. But it was hard.

Gordie was so busy staring at them that he didn't hear Miss Tingle call on him. He was so busy staring at them that he didn't hear the lunch bell ring.

"Gordie, wake up," said Lamont.

Gordie closed his speller and got in line behind Lamont and Red. Lamont was so busy telling Red about the talent show that he didn't even notice when Gordie stopped to tie his shoe. He just kept laughing and walking down the stairs to the cafeteria.

Gordie took his time tying his sneaker. Then he opened his locker and stared at his jacket. Finally he walked over and took a long, long drink from the water fountain. The hall was empty. Nobody even knew he wasn't in the cafeteria. Lamont was probably asking Red if he wanted half of his sandwich.

What was so special about Red anyway? Big, big deal that Red's dog was on TV. Gordie headed down the hall, wishing Scratch could be a little bit more fancy—fancy enough to get Lamont back as a best friend.

Chapter 3

By the time Gordie got down to the cafeteria everyone was already eating lunch. Gordie squeezed in beside Lamont, but there wasn't much room since everyone was gathered around Red like he was a movie star. Gordie opened his lunch bag and grabbed his sandwich so hard his fingers dug into the peanut butter.

Lamont was ordering kids around. "Hey, move back, guys. Give Red some room." Lamont wiggled on the bench and almost shoved Gordie onto the floor. "Can't you see he's trying to eat?"

Gordie shoved his sandwich back into the bag. Lamont was acting like he was a cafeteria lady.

Lucy rolled a meatball down the table. "Here, Red. You can give this to your dog."

"You have to bring your dog to school," said Mikey. "It would make room nine kind of famous."

"Dogs aren't allowed in the school," said Gordie. "Miss Tingle would get fired. Is that what you guys want?"

Lamont didn't even answer Gordie. He started telling Red that he could play the guitar. Gordie knew Lamont didn't really know how to play. Nobody could tell which song it was. All his songs sounded like "Three Blind Mice."

Gordie's stomach was doing jumping jacks. He didn't have a talent. His dog didn't have a talent. It didn't seem fair.

"I'm going to float a paper clip on water," said Jeremy.

"That's a good trick," said Lucy. "What kind of trick is your scaredy-cat dog going to do, Gordie? Maybe he could hide his head in Miss Tingle's trash can."

"Oh, be quiet," said Lamont. He leaned

over and bumped his shoulder against Gordie's. "Scratch is ten times smarter than you."

Lucy closed her eyes. "Fine, show me."

"He will," snapped Lamont. "Maybe Gordie and Red will have their dogs do a trick together, right, Gordie?"

Red nodded. "My dog knows how to jump over barrels and walk backward. But he can't bark to ten or anything like that."

Gordie wished Scratch could count to ten. He wished his dog knew so much math that they'd be the hit of the talent show. He looked up. Everyone was staring at him, waiting for him to prove that Scratch wasn't just a dumb dog. Lamont elbowed him.

"So, what kind of trick can Scratch do, Gordie? Can he bark to three or four?"

Gordie tried to swallow. "Well . . ."

"See," said Lucy. "I told you."

Gordie crinkled up his lunch bag and stood up. "Scratch knows how to do something real hard, Lucy Diaz."

"Like what?" asked Lucy.

"Yeah, tell her, Gordie," said Lamont.

Gordie took a deep breath. "He knows how to count, how to add, how to subtract, and—"

Gordie never got a chance to finish. Everyone was too busy laughing at him, even Lamont.

Chapter
4

As soon as Gordie and Lamont reached the playground, Lamont said, "Don't be mad at me. I didn't mean to laugh at you. But we both know Scratch can't do tricks."

"I know," Gordie said slowly. Scratch didn't even know how to bury a bone. "I'll teach him some tricks real fast."

Lamont nodded. "I'll see if I can come over and help you."

Lucy and Melinda Jones raced over. "Tell Melinda about your dog, Gordie. She doesn't believe you one bit."

Melinda was a fourth-grader who was pretty mean to everyone. Even some of the sixth-grade boys were afraid of her.

"Liars are kicked out of school," snapped

Melinda. She smiled like she loved that rule a lot.

Lamont frowned at Melinda. "Maybe you should be kicked out of school for walking around with all those freckles."

Melinda spun on one foot and marched away. Lucy watched her go.

"Gordie, you can have one of my talents since I have so many. Do you want me to teach you to draw with your eyes closed?"

"No," said Gordie. "Scratch is my talent act."

"Scratch will be the star of the show," added Lamont. "I'm going to go help Gordie with the tricks today after school."

"Hey, Lamont," called Red. He raced over with Mikey and Amon. "Do you want to come over to the television studio with me today?"

Lamont laughed. "Cool. I'll ask my mom."

"We get to come, too," said Mikey.

Red nodded toward Lucy and Gordie. "Next time I'll ask you two to come, but my mom only allows three friends at a time."

"Don't forget to ask me," said -Lucy. "Maybe the TV people will want to put me in a commercial."

Gordie shrugged. "I'll probably be too busy teaching Scratch his tricks." He looked over at Lamont, hoping he would remember about their plans to work with Scratch.

But Lamont must have forgotten. Gordie watched as he raced off across the play-ground with Red and the other boys.

Lucy asked, "Want me to come over and help with Scratch? I love dogs."

Gordie shook his head. "No thanks. I'll get him ready all by myself."

Lucy turned and hurried over to the swing sets.

"Scratch just has to learn two tricks before Friday," muttered Gordie. "Then no one will care about Red's dumb dog."

Gordie smelled peanut butter. He turned around and saw Larry Green. He was stuffing saltine crackers into his mouth.

"Who's Red?" asked Larry. He was in the fourth grade, but he knew kids in every grade. He always ate leftover food from other kids' lunches.

"He's a new kid in our class," said Gordie. "His dog does television commercials. When he brings the dog to the talent show, Red will be the star of third grade."

"What are you going to do for the show?" asked Larry.

"I don't know." Gordie was tired of pretending Scratch knew tricks. Besides, last Sunday Larry had seen a big squirrel chasing Scratch in the park.

"I'd do a back flip," said Larry. "I can do ten in a row."

Gordie dug in his pocket and pulled out a candy bar. "I'll give you this candy bar if you teach me how to do a flip."

"Sure. Come over to the grass." Larry ripped off the wrapper and ate the candy bar in two bites. He handed Gordie the wrapper.

A few fourth-graders came over to watch Larry as he began. Gordie spotted Lamont and Red playing basketball with some fifth-graders. Wait until they saw him doing back flips across the playground.

Gordie felt better already. Once he learned to flip, Scratch could stay home.

Larry stood up and brushed off his pants. "Okay, Gordie, now just put your hands like this. Then make your head look back like this."

Gordie watched Larry do another perfect back flip.

"Okay, Gordie, your turn. Lean your head back and flip."

Larry gave Gordie's back a push. For

one great second, Gordie was in the air. Then he crashed onto his head.

"Good try, kid," said Larry. "Your forehead is grass-stained. Want to try again?"

"No thanks." Gordie brushed the dirt from his hair. What was he going to do now? Gordie rubbed his head. It hurt. Too bad it didn't fall off and roll down the hill. Then Miss Tingle would say he didn't have to be in the show. Then his brother, Doug,

wouldn't be mad when he watched his dumb act.

The recess bell rang. Unless a tornado picked Gordie up and blew him to Ohio, he'd have to teach Scratch a good trick by Friday. And since Lamont was busy with his new best friend, Gordie would have to do it by himself.

Chapter
5

Gordie hopped off the bus. Scratch was busy digging a big hole in Mrs. Yurcon's front yard. Gordie hurried over. Mrs. Yurcon usually turned the hose on Scratch when he started ruining her yard.

"You have the worst-behaved dog in the world," she would shout as Scratch raced around the yard, barking at the hose.

"Come here, boy," called Gordie. He got down on the grass and hugged his dog. "Want to go to school with me on Friday? Want to show my class how smart you are?"

Scratch licked Gordie's ear.

"Lucy has a zillion talents," said Gordie. "And Lamont thinks the new kid in school is real cool. Cooler than me."

"Hey, Shrimp," said Doug. He tapped Gordie on the head with his baseball cap. "Want to go to the park with Miller and me and hit some balls?"

"I have to get ready for the talent show, Doug. I have to teach Scratch two tricks. He's my talent."

Scratch rolled on his back. His four skinny legs waved in the air.

Doug laughed. "Hey, pretty good trick. Use that in the act."

"The tricks have to be hard," explained Gordie. "Hard enough to make the fifth-graders clap."

Doug shook his head. "I don't know, Shrimp. My class didn't even clap when the weather man from channel four came to our room."

Gordie looked down at Scratch as he dug his nose into the grass.

"If I were you, I'd get a new act," said Doug. "Especially since that new kid has a famous dog. I can hardly wait to see him."

For the next ten minutes, Gordie tried

to see how many tricks Scratch knew how to do.

He didn't know how to do any.

Mom came out the back door with peanut butter on crackers. "If you aren't coming inside for your snack, I'd better bring it to you."

"Thanks, Mom." Gordie scrambled up and took a cracker.

Scratch sniffed the air, then charged over, barking. He sat down by Gordie's feet and wagged his tail. Gordie tossed him a tiny bite.

"That dog will do anything for food," said Mom.

"I know," said Gordie. "Especially peanut butter."

Before Mom went inside, she picked up a tennis ball and threw it across the hedge. Scratch took off after the ball. He raced around the side of the house. When Scratch returned, he didn't have the tennis ball in his mouth. He had Mrs. Yurcon's yellow garden gloves. Mrs. Yurcon chased after Scratch.

"Give me back those gloves, you dumb dog," she cried.

"Sorry, Mrs. Yurcon," said Gordie. "I'm teaching him to fetch."

"Teach him some manners instead," she said, and then went back to her yard.

Gordie shook his head. "Now pay attention, Scratch. You have to learn some tricks."

Gordie shared his snack with Scratch and then tried to teach him to roll over. Gordie rolled the dog down the side of the yard. Scratch just waited for Gordie to roll him. No one in room 9 would clap for that trick. Lumpy Labriola would get all the fifth-grade boys to boo.

Gordie sighed and lay down next to his dog. Scratch's tummy growled. Scratch liked food as much as Larry Green.

Gordie stood up fast. He had an idea. Scratch would learn tricks faster with a secret weapon—and the weapon was right inside Gordie's kitchen.

Chapter
6

Gordie raced inside his house and pulled open the pantry door.

"Yippee," he said. He grabbed a large jar of peanut butter and hurried back outside. Scratch was busy chasing the neighbor's cat around the garage.

"Come here, boy," Gordie called. As soon as he took the lid off the peanut butter and waved it around, Scratch came galloping over.

Gordie and Scratch worked hard all afternoon. It took half a jar of peanut butter to teach Scratch two tricks.

After dinner, Gordie showed off his magical dog. "Watch this, Doug. Sit!"

Scratch sat down. Gordie gave his dog

a spoonful of peanut butter. Scratch licked the spoon clean.

"Cool," said Doug.

"Watch this one," said Gordie. "It's harder. Okay, now, speak!"

Scratch barked. Gordie got a new spoon and held out another spoonful of peanut butter.

"What do you think of my act for the talent show, Doug?"

Doug shook his head. "Well, Shrimp. I don't want to burst your bubble, but I don't think it's good enough. You're up against a television dog."

Gordie thumped down the peanut butter jar.

Doug picked up his backpack and pulled out his math book. "Now, if you could teach Scratch how to do my math homework, he'd be the star of the show."

Scratch thumped his tail and laid his head on Doug's knee.

"Sure," Gordie muttered. "Teach Scratch how to add and subtract by Friday. No problem. It took half a jar of peanut butter to teach Scratch two little tricks."

Scratch closed his eyes and whined, like he was sad he knew only dumb tricks.

"You'll think of something," said Doug. "And I'll pay Lumpy not to boo you."

Gordie smiled. He had the best big brother. "Doug, will you clap for me for free?"

"Yeah. I'll get my friends to clap for you, too."

"Thanks." Gordie watched as Doug worked on a math sheet. "Is that hard?" he asked.

"Yeah, it is. I hate to subtract really big numbers."

Gordie loved math. In fact, he loved it so much that he thought it was easy. He sat down and patted Scratch, wondering how hard it would be to teach a dog to add.

"Gordie," Mom called. "Telephone call."

Gordie darted to the phone. "Hello?"

"Gordie, it's me," said Lamont. "Hey, sorry I forgot to come over today."

"That's okay," said Gordie. "I taught Scratch two tricks and—"

"You won't believe how cute Red's dog is," Lamont said. "His dog is named Lawrence. He doesn't have to sleep outside in a doghouse because he has his own bedroom. He has this fluffy cushion and. . . ." Lamont stopped to catch his breath. "Anyway, their house is cool and his mom let us order an extra-large pizza and wings. She said we could order anything we wanted, and we didn't even have a coupon."

Gordie chewed his lip. His mom always made them use coupons for pizza, but she never ordered a pepperoni pizza when Lamont was visiting. Everyone knew Lamont hated pepperoni.

"Red wants to know if I can sleep over at his house on Saturday, but I told him that we were supposed to go fishing with your uncle Leo." Lamont cleared his throat. "So, my mom said I should call you."

Gordie smiled. "Yeah, Uncle Leo said we could bring the tent and sleep out if you want. He'll tell us the best stories about being chased by bears and crazy raccoons—"

Lamont cleared his throat again. "Yeah, well I think I heard those stories last time. So, anyway, Red asked me to sleep over since his dad is taking everyone to Cleveland for a Cavs basketball game and . . ." Lamont was quiet. "So, I guess I can't go fishing with you and Uncle Leo. Is that cool with you?"

Gordie nodded. It took another two seconds before he could make his voice strong enough to say, "Oh, sure."

Chapter 7

By the time Gordie went upstairs to his bedroom, he was more mad than sad. Lamont wasn't a best friend at all. He was a crummy friend. Gordie sat on the side of his bed and wondered who he should ask to go fishing. He'd ask someone right in front of Lamont. He would ask someone in a loud voice and then high-five him. Gordie flopped over on his bed and pulled his pillow over his head.

Doug walked into the room and tossed his backpack into the corner. "Finished my math. Want to go shoot hoops with me?"

"No thanks," Gordie mumbled from underneath the pillow.

Doug pulled the pillow away and

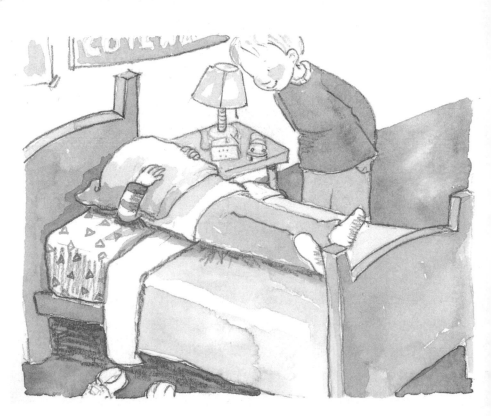

swatted Gordie. "Hey, don't sweat the talent show. You'll think of something."

Gordie sat up. "Sure, all I have to do is teach Scratch how to add and subtract. No problem."

"Gordie Barr!" Mom hollered up the stairs.

Gordie hopped off the bed. Mom only used both names when he was in trouble. "What, Mom?"

Mom walked up the stairs, holding the peanut butter jar. "Did you give Scratch this jar to play with?"

Scratch peeked out from behind Mom's jeans. He had peanut butter smeared all over his whiskers.

"No, I set the jar on the table." Gordie tried not to smile.

Mom tried not to smile back. She handed Gordie the jar. "Here you go. This jar probably has fleas in it. You can use the rest of it to train this silly dog."

Scratch raced into Gordie's room, licking his whiskers. Gordie hurried back into his room and put the peanut butter on his dresser. "Sit, Scratch."

Scratch sat down, his eyes glued to the jar. Gordie paced. There just had to be a way to get Scratch to do a great trick using peanut butter.

Doug held up a deck of cards. "Want to play cards?"

Scratch got up and jumped on Doug's bed, licking the cards. Doug held the deck

up, laughing. "You can't eat the cards, Scratch."

Gordie smiled, then stood frozen in the middle of the room. He looked at the deck of cards and then back to the peanut butter jar.

"I've got it, Doug!" said Gordie. "I think I know how to teach Scratch to do math."

"Then you'll be the star of the show," said Doug. "Scratch will be the smartest dog in the whole world."

Gordie took the cards from Doug and laid them next to the peanut butter. He didn't care if Scratch was the smartest dog in the world. He just had to be better than Red's dog. Gordie picked up the cards and counted them. Fifty-two. Gordie counted out four cards. That was all he would need to make Scratch the star of the third-grade talent show.

Chapter 8

Gordie could hardly wait to get to school. He'd tell Miss Tingle about his new act. Then he'd ask Mikey to go fishing with Uncle Leo. Gordie walked to his locker. Last night he had tried to teach Scratch to add using the playing cards. Scratch was hard to teach. He kept trying to eat the cards. When Gordie lost his temper and said, "Don't eat these, Scratch!" the dog crawled under the bed.

Gordie hung his jacket in his locker. He looked down the hall and saw Red and Lamont laughing by the water fountain. Gordie slammed his locker and walked inside room 9. Just wait until they saw Scratch's trick. The only problem was, the

show was in three days. That didn't leave much time.

As soon as Gordie slid into his seat, Mikey walked in.

"Hey, Mikey, come over here," called Gordie.

"Hi, Gordie. Only three more days till the big show."

Gordie tried not to frown. "Don't remind me. Hey, do you want to go fishing with me and my uncle Leo on Saturday? He's cool and . . ."

Mikey's face got a little red, and he started bending a paper clip back and forth. "Gosh, that sounds fun, but . . ." Mikey looked over his shoulder at Red and Lamont, who were making a lot of noise by the globe. "Red asked me to go to a basketball game in—"

"Cleveland," said Gordie. Was Red's dad taking the whole third grade to the basketball game?

Lamont came over and knocked his knuckles on Gordie's head. "Anybody home?"

Lamont had been knocking on Gordie's head since kindergarten. Gordie usually laughed. But not today.

"Leave me alone," he snapped. He shook Lamont's hand away and opened his desk. He stared inside, wishing a fire alarm would ring so everyone would have to run outside. He would keep on running, straight to his house.

"What a grouch," muttered Lamont. He slid into his own seat.

Once the morning bell rang, Gordie had a hard time concentrating. Miss Tingle was excited about the talent show. She let the whole class skip spelling so they could make tickets for the fifth-graders. Gordie wanted to raise his hand and tell Miss Tingle that he couldn't do the show after all. But he knew she wouldn't believe him. Besides, Gordie had already told a big lie. He had told everyone that his dog knew tricks.

When Miss Tingle announced it was time for lunch, Gordie tapped Lamont on the arm. "Want to eat lunch together?"

47

Lamont shrugged. "Yeah, sure." Lamont leaned over to Red. "You ready for lunch?"

Red smiled and held up a big paper bag. "I had my mom pack an extra pepperoni and cheese sandwich for you, Lamont."

Gordie waited for Lamont to tell Red that he hated pepperoni. He hated it so much that Gordie never ordered it on his pizza so Lamont wouldn't even have to smell it.

Lamont looked over at Gordie, then turned back to Red. "Great."

Gordie grabbed his bag and hurried to line up. Lamont was busy talking to Red. Lamont was acting like a big faker. Maybe he would go ahead and eat the pepperoni and throw up all over the cafeteria.

"Want to eat lunch together, Mikey?" asked Gordie.

Mikey was busy balancing raisins on his closed eyes, but he said, "Okay."

Lunch wasn't as much fun eating with Mikey. He spent more time playing with his food. He ripped the crust off his bread and then rolled his cheese sandwich into tiny balls.

"Don't they look like snowballs?" asked Mikey as he made a tiny cheese-sandwich snowman.

Gordie kept watching Lamont, waiting for him to throw up. He saw Lamont hide bits of pepperoni inside his lunch bag whenever Red wasn't looking.

By the time school was over, Gordie had a huge headache. His head hurt so much he was afraid it would crack open and his brain would bounce out like a rubber ball. Gordie hopped off the bus. He wasn't looking forward to teaching Scratch math tricks.

When Gordie walked into the kitchen, Scratch was asleep under the table.

"Your dog spent the entire day trying to jump onto your dresser to get to the peanut butter, Gordie," said Mom. She put a plate of sliced apples on the table. "I finally had to close your bedroom door."

"Sorry, Mom."

Gordie handed Mom his math sheet. "I got them all right."

Mom kissed Gordie's head and stuck the

math page onto the refrigerator. "You are such a math whiz."

Doug walked in and tossed his backpack onto the floor. "Is that pizza I smell?"

Mom smiled and opened the oven. "Pepperoni."

"Great!" said Doug.

Gordie stared at the pepperoni and felt bad. He thought of how sick Lamont had looked after lunch. Miss Tingle had told him to go down to the nurse's room and lie on the hard green couch.

"I'm not hungry, Mom," Gordie said as he walked upstairs.

Scratch moaned and followed Gordie up the stairs. The dog slumped down on the floor as Gordie lined up the cards. Gordie held up two cards. "Okay, Scratch. Now pay attention. What do you get when you add the three of clubs to the four of diamonds?"

Scratch leaned over and licked Gordie's sneaker.

"Okay, how about this." Gordie held out the three of clubs and the four of dia-

monds. "If I add one and two, what do I get?" Gordie held the two cards in front of Scratch's nose.

Scratch licked the four of diamonds.

"No!" cried Gordie. He waved the three of clubs. "It's this one!"

Scratch scrambled to his feet and ran out of the room.

Gordie raced after him. "Sorry, boy. Come back here. I won't yell at you again."

Scratch raced into the bathroom and jumped into the tub.

Gordie skidded to a stop. He really must be a grouch if Scratch would rather have a bath than be with him. Gordie hurried back into his room and stuck his finger in the peanut butter. He went back into the bathroom and let Scratch lick it off. Gordie smiled and held out the two cards. "Now, try again, buddy."

Scratch licked the three of clubs.

"Great!" Gordie hugged his dog. "You did it. Now, try this. What is two and two?"

Scratch licked the three of clubs again.

Gordie tried to keep the smile on his

face. "No, boy. It's the four of diamonds, not the three of clubs. Try again."

Scratch licked the three of clubs and then swallowed it.

"Hey!" Gordie pried open Scratch's mouth and pulled out the card. It was wet and mushy and . . . and it smelled like peanut butter. Gordie smelled his left hand. It still had peanut butter on it. He must have gotten it on the three of clubs and that's why Scratch kept licking it. So if Gordie wanted Scratch to pick a certain card, he just had to use the secret weapon . . . peanut butter.

"Yippee," cried Gordie. He hurried out into the hall and got the rest of the playing cards. "Come on, Scratch. Turning you into a math whiz is going to be a snap. Red's dog is going to look like a kindergarten dog next to you."

Chapter
9

Gordie worked with Scratch every minute he could. It took another jar of peanut butter, but the act was going great. On Friday morning, Gordie could hardly wait to get to school.

Gordie raced into the kitchen. Doug handed him a bagel. "Here, hurry up or we'll miss the bus, Shrimp. Don't want to be late for the big show."

Gordie slid into his seat and drank his juice. "Scratch is going to be great."

"Show me your trick now," said Doug.

Gordie shook his head. "You have to wait. Just make sure your friends clap for me."

"They will. I had to give Lumpy a quarter but Hoover only charged me a dime.

They'll clap real loud. And they won't boo you, not even if you stink."

"Thanks, Doug." Gordie reached down and patted Scratch. "Mom, make sure you don't feed Scratch this morning. He has to be real hungry for the show."

"Aye, aye, sir," said Mom. "I'll even give him a bath." Mom glanced at the clock. "Take the bagels with you, boys. Time to catch the bus. Scratch and I will see you at one o'clock."

Gordie got up and shoved the peanut butter jar and playing cards into his backpack. Scratch got up and sniffed Gordie's backpack, wagging his tail.

"Not now, boy," said Gordie. "It's almost showtime!"

Chapter
10

Lamont wasn't on the bus that morning. Gordie wasn't surprised. Lamont had driven to school with Red's dad for the past three days. Red lived a block away and he said Lamont could ride to school with him so he could sleep an extra twenty minutes.

Gordie leaned against the bus window. He tried not to look sad that he had to sit next to a sixth-grade girl who kept cracking her gum and yelling to her friends two rows back.

When Gordie hurried into room 9, Miss Tingle handed him a cupcake. "Good morning, Gordie. I brought treats since it's our talent-show day. Are you excited?"

"Yes, my mom is giving Scratch a bath so he won't leave fleas in your room."

Miss Tingle patted Gordie's back. "Great. We'll have two dogs in third grade today. Red's mother said Lawrence will be here at one. I hope the dogs get along."

Gordie shrugged. "Scratch loves everyone. Except Mrs. Cillo's cat."

As more and more kids arrived, Gordie started to get nervous. Half of him was excited. The other half was worried that Scratch might not want any peanut butter today. Or he might decide that Lawrence looked like Mrs. Cillo's cat and chase him all over the school.

Lamont rushed in with Red. They were talking about how cool the basketball game was going to be. Gordie didn't care. He was going to have lots of fun fishing. Uncle Leo had said that Gordie could bring Scratch instead of Lamont. Gordie was already planning to bring pepperoni sandwiches for lunch. Maybe fifty. Lamont wouldn't be there to smell them.

When the lunch bell rang in room 9, everyone cheered. Right after lunch, the talent show would get started. Gordie stood in line for lunch by himself. He didn't want to eat with Mikey anymore. Yesterday Mikey had had a cream cheese and olive sandwich. But instead of eating it, Mikey had pasted the little green olive slices all over his face.

"Look, I have the olive pox!" Mikey had yelled.

Today, Gordie didn't care if he ate alone. He wanted to think about his act.

But when Lamont asked, "Want to eat lunch with Red and me?" Gordie said okay.

At lunch Gordie mostly listened to Red brag about things. He bragged ten times more than Lucy. Gordie stared at Lamont, wondering if Lamont still thought Red was cool.

"Wait till you see Lawrence," said Red. "My mom has this leather leash with his initials burned into it. Must have cost a hundred bucks."

Gordie took a tiny bite of baloney and hoped his mom could find Scratch's green leash. Sometimes when she couldn't find it, she just used part of a clothesline.

Instead of room 9's going out for recess, they waited until Miss Tingle came down and got them from the cafeteria. It was finally showtime.

Miss Tingle walked everyone back upstairs and helped kids with their costumes. Lamont ran around the room. He wanted everyone to see his fake mustache.

"Do I look forty years old, Gordie?" asked Lamont.

"You look fifty or sixty," said Gordie. He wondered if he should have a mustache. Maybe not. Scratch might not know it was him. Gordie didn't want his dog barking at him. The fifth-graders might boo.

"Where's Scratch?" Lamont asked.

"He's coming at one o'clock. He needs to rest."

"Gordie, how come you won't tell me about your act? Are you afraid I'll tell Red?"

Gordie shook his head. "No, it's just that I want it to be a surprise. I haven't told anyone."

"But, we're best friends, aren't we?" Lamont's mustache wiggled around like he was upset.

"I guess. I mean, you're Red's best friend now."

Lamont frowned at Gordie. Then he looked over at Red. "He has lots of stuff. His own television and—"

Miss Tingle flashed the lights. "Five more minutes, ladies and gentlemen. Are we ready?"

Gordie slid back into his seat. Lamont hadn't answered Gordie's question. Was Red now Lamont's best friend? He stared up at the clock. His mom would be walking in the door in ten minutes. He hoped Scratch would be hungry.

Lucy skipped over to Gordie's desk. She twirled around. "How do I look?"

"Good," said Gordie. Lucy was wearing a pink ballet dress. She looked like she'd just jumped out of a little jewelry box.

"Lucy, why are you wearing that?" asked Lamont. "I thought you were going to draw a picture with your eyes shut."

"I am," said Lucy. She spun around again. "I am a ballerina girl who can draw."

Miss Tingle clapped her hands. Gordie thought she looked extra pretty. She had more curls on her head.

"I know we are all excited about the show. But sit down now. We want to get ready for our audience to arrive."

Gordie reached under his desk and got his backpack. He reached in and got the playing cards. He hid the peanut butter in his desk. He didn't want anyone to see his secret weapon.

Gordie looked around the room. Everyone was smiling, anxious for the show to begin. Was Gordie the only one in room 9 who wondered if his act would go all right?

Soon the parents started to arrive. Lucy and Billy gave them programs. Gordie knew his act was the seventh. He'd go on after Lamont. Red's dog was going to be

last. Miss Tingle was saving him for the big act, like a fireworks display.

The fifth-graders came into the room. Some fifth-graders sat on the radiator until their teacher, Mr. Johnson, yelled at them. Then everyone sat on the floor and tried to be good.

Red's mom arrived with Lawrence. The dog was short, with shiny golden hair. Gordie thought it was a cocker spaniel. Scratch was a little bit cocker spaniel. He was a little bit of a lot of dogs. Lawrence wore a diamond collar. Gordie bit his lip. Scratch's collar was pretty old. It had come for free inside a bag of dog biscuits.

"Wow, cool dog!" said Mikey. "Can I have his autograph?"

Parents and kids laughed. One fifth-grader leaned over and patted Lawrence's leg. The dog jumped back and barked. Red's mom yanked back on the leash, hard.

Gordie leaned back in his seat. Had that hurt the dog? His mom never hurt Scratch.

Not even when he snuck onto the living room couch and drooled.

More and more parents came in and sat on the small chairs in the back. Gordie looked around the room. Doug smiled and gave him the thumbs-up sign. That made Gordie feel a little better. Lumpy looked over at Gordie and held up a quarter.

Lamont's mother came in. She took a picture of Lamont. Then she said, "Gordie, come over here so I can take a picture of you and Lamont." Gordie stood next to Lamont, but he didn't smile. Neither did Lamont. Maybe Lamont was afraid his mustache would fall off. Or, maybe he was mad that Red wasn't in the picture.

Room 9 was getting filled up. There were only two empty chairs in the back. Gordie got up and peeked into the hall. Where was Mom? Where was Scratch?

"Hey, Gordie," whispered Doug. "Where's Mom?"

"I don't know." Gordie looked down at his cards. What if Mom didn't come?

Scratch hated baths. Maybe he'd jumped out of the tub and run off.

Miss Tingle flashed the lights on and off. The show was about to begin.

Gordie kept his head down. Without Scratch, Gordie didn't have an act. And without an act, he'd be kicked out of the show.

Miss Tingle walked to the front of the room. "Thank you for coming to our show."

"You're welcome," called out a fifth-grader.

"We will start our talent show with Lucy Diaz," said Miss Tingle. "Lucy will draw a bird while wearing a blindfold."

Miss Tingle blindfolded Lucy. Then she handed her a big black marker.

Lucy drew a pretty good bird. One eye was not on its head. It floated beside the bird like a little black balloon.

A fifth-grader laughed. Doug leaned over and poked him. Gordie was glad his brother was here.

Gordie looked at the closed door. No Mom. No Scratch.

Billy went next. Then David, Tomeka, and Amy. Finally Miss Tingle called Lamont's name. He played the guitar and sang. The fifth-graders whistled and clapped.

Gordie's hands started to sweat. He was next! Maybe he could tell Miss Tingle he had to throw up. She would send him to the nurse's room, and he could lie on the couch until the show was over.

Gordie's heart was pounding so hard he was sure everyone could hear it. He was about to cover his ears when the door to room 9 opened.

Chapter
11

Scratch burst into the room, pulling Gordie's mom with him.

"Hey, Doug, your dog's taking your mom for a walk," Lumpy called out.

When Scratch heard Doug's name, his head jerked up and he tried to pull Mom through the crowd. Mom dug her heels down and held tightly.

"Is that the TV star?" asked a fifth-grader.

"No," said her friend. "That's just a regular old dog."

Scratch sat down and scratched behind his left ear.

"Fleabag," whispered a fifth-grader.

Gordie was glad when Doug leaned over and shushed the kid.

"Sorry, Miss Tingle," said Mom. "When I got to school, Scratch jumped out and a squirrel chased him."

"Maybe your dog is a chicken instead of a dog," said Red.

"Settle down, please," said Miss Tingle. "Gordie and his dog will be next."

Gordie stood up. He put his playing cards in one hand and walked to the front of the room. Scratch licked Gordie's hand and followed him. Gordie bowed. He pointed to Scratch. "Today you will meet the smartest dog in the world."

"If he's so smart, what's the capital of Ohio?" called out Lucy.

Lots of kids laughed. Lamont clapped and nodded his head.

"Let's give Gordie our attention," said Miss Tingle.

Gordie nodded and started his act. "Sit, Scratch." Scratch sat down. He was staring at the playing cards. His tongue hung out.

Gordie pulled the cards from his pocket. He held them up in the air. "My dog will now answer an addition problem."

Gordie walked to the board. He printed: $4+3=\underline{\quad}$.

"Okay, Scratch. Four plus three equals what?" Gordie held the playing cards up again. "I have a seven of hearts and a three of clubs. Which is it, Scratch?"

Scratch sniffed both cards. Then he licked the seven of hearts.

Gordie held up the seven of hearts. Everyone clapped.

"Now for the hard question," said Gordie. "Only a few dogs in the world can do subtraction." Gordie printed: $12-5=\underline{\quad}$ on the board. "Twelve minus five is what, Scratch?"

Scratch sniffed both cards. Then he licked the seven of hearts. He licked it again, and then bit down hard on it.

Gordie pulled it from Scratch's mouth. He held the wet card up in the air.

"Yes, twelve minus five equals seven."

Everyone clapped. A few fifth-graders whistled. Gordie found Doug in the crowd. He gave Gordie the thumbs-up sign.

"How'd you do that?" asked Lucy. "Let me see those cards!"

Gordie's hand closed around the playing cards. He didn't want Lucy to discover his secret weapon.

"Your dog isn't that smart," said Red. "He's only doing second-grade math."

"Yeah," added Lumpy. "It's not like Scratch knows how to read."

A few kids laughed, but they stopped right away when Mr. Johnson stood up and frowned at Lumpy.

"Scratch loves to read," Gordie said slowly. It was true, sort of. Whenever Gordie read aloud, Scratch would lie down beside him, like he was listening. Gordie smiled, remembering how Scratch thumped his tail when Gordie changed his voice as he read.

Miss Tingle smiled at Gordie. "Does Scratch have a favorite story?"

Gordie tried to think fast. Everyone was watching him.

"Dogs can't read," muttered Red.

Gordie patted the dog's head. Scratch wasn't the smartest dog in the world, but he wasn't a dope, either.

Dope . . . dopey. Gordie smiled. He knew what he would say.

"Scratch loves *Snow White,* Miss Tingle. He knows all about that book."

Miss Tingle looked surprised. "He does?"

"Sure," Gordie said. "And he can prove it."

"No dog can understand a book," said Red.

"Scratch can," said Gordie. He cleared his throat and led Scratch back to the chalkboard. "My dog needs his own library card."

Lots of kids laughed.

"Sure . . ." Gordie's hand closed around his cards. "Scratch, remember how much you liked *Snow White*?"

Scratch sat down and scratched behind his left ear.

Red shook his head. "Yeah, right."

Gordie held out both playing cards. "How many dwarves did Snow White live with, Scratch?"

Gordie pushed the cards closer to Scratch. Come on, boy, thought Gordie. You can do it.

"I know how many," said a tall fifth-grade girl with red hair. "I can name them all. There's Bashful and Happy and—"

Miss Tingle held up her hand. "Let Scratch answer."

"How many dwarves?" Gordie asked quietly.

Scratch lowered his head and then licked the seven of hearts.

"Way to go, Scratch," called Doug.

"Nice trick," added Mr. Johnson. When he started clapping, the rest of the audience joined in. When Lumpy whistled, no one even yelled at him.

"Good job, Gordie," said Miss Tingle. "Take a bow!"

As Gordie bent down, Scratch reached over and grabbed the seven of hearts. With one chomp, the card disappeared.

Gordie tried not to laugh. Now nobody would discover the peanut butter smeared on the back of the card.

"Wow!" said Miss Tingle. "Scratch is quite a dog. He made the card disappear! Scratch knows math and magic."

"I love your magic dog," Lucy called out.

Gordie put Scratch on his leash and they sat down and watched the rest of the show. During the next act, Scratch yawned and fell asleep. Gordie kept his arm around him and watched the show.

Miss Tingle clapped after Mikey played "Jingle Bells" using only his nose. "Now, we are all very lucky to have a chance to meet Lawrence, the television dog."

Gordie watched as the fifth-graders got real quiet.

Red got out of his seat and took the leather leash from his mother.

"Come on, boy," said Red. The dog trotted after Red to the center of the room. "My dog is going to sit, kneel, roll over, and then do a flip in the air."

Lumpy Labriola whistled twice. Then his teacher leaned over and said something loudly in his ear.

"My dog is used to being around professionals, so please try not to get yelled at during his act," said Red. "And don't take flash pictures."

Mr. Johnson lowered his camera and frowned at Red.

Gordie leaned forward and watched as Lawrence sat, knelt, rolled over, and then stood up, ready for the flip.

"Try to remain quiet," said Red. He looked stern.

Mr. Johnson stood up and snapped his fingers at his class. "I don't want to hear a word. Pay attention." He gave one final snap. Everyone sat up straighter, even the adults.

Lawrence swung his sleek head toward Mr. Johnson. He sat down and hung his head.

Red jerked on Lawrence's leash. The dog's head swung up, then struggled against the leash.

Red's mother leaned over and swatted the dog under its chin. The kids in the room started to squirm. Red's cheeks got pink.

"Why do they hit the dog?" whispered Lamont.

"He usually doesn't do this," said Red's mother. "The dog is a professional."

Scratch scrambled to his feet, wagging his tail.

Gordie watched as Red and his mother tried to calm down Lawrence. The dog was prancing around in a tiny circle, pulling on his leash. A few of the fifth-graders started to laugh.

"Class, let's settle down," said Miss Tingle. She looked at the light switch like she wanted to flash the lights.

"Can I start my act over?" asked Red.

"I feel sick," called out Mikey.

Lawrence started barking at Mikey. Red jerked the leash. Gordie was out of his seat before he knew it. He had the jar of peanut butter in his hand. "Here, Red. Offer your dog some of this. Scratch loves it."

Red stared at Gordie. "Peanut butter?"

Gordie nodded, scooping out a fingerful and offering it to Lawrence. Lawrence backed away, then sat down. Gordie leaned closer. Red patted Lawrence on the head. "Go on, boy. I love peanut butter, too."

Lawrence looked up at Red, then gently licked the peanut butter from Gordie's finger. Scratch scurried up the aisle, sniffing the air. Doug hopped up and tried to grab Scratch. But Scratch raced over to Lawrence, his tail going faster than windshield wipers.

"Get your dog away from Lawrence," snapped Red.

"It's okay. Scratch loves everyone," said Gordie. "Except squirrels and Mrs. Cillo's cat."

Red shook his head. "I don't know. . . ."

Gordie patted Scratch. "Sit down, Scratch."

Scratch sat, then he stuck out his long tongue and licked a small bit of peanut butter from Lawrence's face.

Lawrence blinked, then slid down and rolled over.

The entire room started to laugh. Miss Tingle started to clap and then everyone joined in. Lumpy stood up and whistled.

Gordie pulled Scratch back and hugged him. Red smiled at Gordie and then knelt down and hugged Lawrence, too.

When everyone stopped clapping, Lucy stood up. "Since Gordie got two turns, can I do a second act?"

"Sure, Lucy, go ahead," called out Lamont. "Gordie and I are still waiting for you to disappear."

Lucy shook her fist at Lamont, but she was smiling. Gordie stood up and clapped his hands. Scratch followed him back to his seat.

"Man, Scratch is the coolest dog in the world," said Lamont. He raised his hand halfway up for a high five, but then he stopped.

"You're not so bad yourself," said Gordie. He kept one hand on Scratch's head and with the other he met Lamont's in

a loud high five. Scratch sat down and thumped his tail.

Miss Tingle thanked everyone for coming and then took the wrap off a huge sheet cake. Lamont's mom served punch in paper cups. The fifth-grade teacher, Mr. Johnson, allowed the fifth-graders to play hangman on the board with the third-graders.

Red walked back to Gordie's desk.

"Thanks for the peanut butter, Gordie," said Red. "I don't know why Lawrence got stage fright. He's used to being in front of lights and cameras."

"But not lots of fifth-graders," added Lamont. "Scratch is used to them because of Gordie's brother, Doug."

Red grinned. "Looks like our dogs like each other."

"Yeah." Gordie kept his face against Scratch's head. Why did he feel so mean all of a sudden? It was probably because Scratch liked Lawrence, but Gordie didn't like Red. Maybe it was easier for dogs to be nice.

Gordie and Red waited by the chalkboard with their dogs while the fifth-graders filed out of room 9.

"Fifth-graders, quiet in the hall," announced Mr. Johnson. As he passed the dogs, he gave them each a pat on the head. "Nice job, boys."

Gordie wasn't sure if Mr. Johnson was talking to them or the dogs.

Red handed Gordie the peanut butter. "Thanks, Gordie. I won't tell anyone about the secret weapon. Not even Lamont."

Gordie looked over at Lamont. Lamont gave him a thumbs-up sign. "That's okay. You can tell Lamont. He's . . . he's my best friend."

Red nodded. "I know. He told me that about ten times."

"He did?" Gordie smiled.

"I had a best friend at my old school," said Red. "Jack is really funny."

"Maybe he can come and visit you sometime," said Gordie.

"Maybe," said Red. But he sounded like Jack wouldn't visit.

"Lawrence has an audition at the television studio," said Red's mom.

Red handed the leash to his mother. "Thanks, Mom."

After Red's dog left, Gordie walked back to his seat. Lamont had his hand up in the air. "Way to go, Gordie. Slap me five."

Gordie and Lamont high-fived.

Lamont sniffed his hand. "Hey, I smell like peanut butter."

Gordie sniffed his own hand and laughed.

"I guess this makes us peanut-butter blood brothers," said Lamont. He looked up at Gordie and grinned.

Gordie grinned back. "Peanut-butter blood brothers best friends."

Gordie held up his hand and Lamont met his with the loudest high-five of all.

Resources

National Information Center
    for Children and Youth
    with Disabilities
P.O. Box 1492
Washington, D.C. 20013
800-695-0285
202-884-8200
www.nichcy.org

President's Committee on
    Mental Retardation
Aerospace Center Building
370 L'Enfant Promenade, S.W.
Suite 701
Washington, D.C. 20447
202-619-0634
www.acf.dhhs.gov/programs/pcmr

National Center for Learning
    Disabilities (NCLD)
381 Park Avenue South
Suite 1401
New York, NY 10016
888-575-7373
212-545-7510
www.ncld.org

National Parent to Parent
    Support and Information
    System, Inc.
P.O. Box 907
Blue Ridge, GA 30513
706-374-3822
www.nppsis.org

Resources

National Down Syndrome
  Society
  666 Broadway
  New York, NY 10012
  800-221-4602
  212-460-9330
  www.ndss.org

Council for Exceptional
  Children (CEC)
  1920 Association Drive
  Reston, VA 20191
  703-620-3660
  888-CEC-SPED
  www.cec.sped.org

Family Village
  Waisman Center
  University of Wisconsin-Madison
  1500 Highland Avenue
  Madison, WI 53705
  608-263-5776
  www.familyvillage.wisc.edu

Administration on
  Developmental Disabilities
  U.S. Department of Health and
  Human Services
  Aerospace Center Building
  370 L'Enfant Promenade, S.W.
  No. 300-F
  Washington, D.C. 20447
  202-690-6590
  www.acf.dhhs.gov/programs/add

National Parent Network
  on Disabilities
  1130 17th Street, N.W.
  Suite 400
  Washington, D.C. 20036
  202-463-2299
  www.npnd.org

Resources

The following organizations can provide information and help.

Special Olympics
  1325 G Street, N.W., Suite 500
  Washington, D.C. 20005
  202-628-3630
  www.specialolympics.org

Best Buddies International
  100 SE Second Street
  Suite 1990
  Miami, FL 33131
  800-89-BUDDY
  305-374-2233
  www.bestbuddies.org

American Association on
  Mental Retardation
  444 North Capitol Street, N.W.
  Suite 846
  Washington, D.C. 20001
  800-424-3688
  202-387-1968
  www.aamr.org

The Arc of the United States
  National Headquaters
  1010 Wayne Avenue
  Suite 650
  Silver Spring, MD 20910
  301-565-3842
  www.info@thearc.org

National Down Syndrome
  Congress
  7000 Peachtree-Dunwoody
  Road, N.E.
  Building #5, Suite 100
  Atlanta, GA 30328
  800-232-NDSC
  770-604-9500
  www.ndsccenter.org

Kate finished her cereal and kissed her mom good-bye. She paused at the door. ❧ "Mom, I think Timmy and I are going to be friends for a long time, too. I can just feel it. And you know what else? If anyone ever asks me 'What's wrong with Timmy?'...I'm going to smile and say, 'Why, nothing...nothing at all!'"

"I sure did, baby, and I learned a lot about friendship and family from that relationship. Tina, Rosie, and I ended up doing lots of things together, like going to the movies and shopping. And you know what? Rosie's disability didn't keep her from being an excellent student. Lots of times she helped Tina and me with our homework. Today, Rosie lives in her own home and is a successful lawyer."   "When Timmy grows up, will he be able to have a job and own his own house?" asked Kate.

Her mother smiled. "If Timmy has those goals, I'm sure he'll be able to do wonderful things just like you. You see, Kate, when each of us looks at someone like Timmy, we should look at the things he *can* do. . . not at what he *can't* do. I believe you two can have a great friendship because you're truly more alike than you are different."

reminded me of something my friend Tina once told me. She said that as she got older, she stopped wishing for a sister who could walk, and she stopped worrying about what other kids might think or say. She realized she loved Rosie just the way she was. After all, she told me, Rosie was always loving, kind, honest, funny, and very loyal. She was also the first to cheer for her and the last to get mad at her. What sister could ask for more?" ❧ "What about you, Mom? Did you ever become friends with Rosie?"

Her mom continued, "You see, sweetheart, no one is perfect. We all have to realize that God loves us just as we are. Even though it may sometimes seem as if there are lots of things wrong with us, I don't think God sees it that way. I think God makes us all different and special. All we have to do is be ourselves, and God will help us make a big difference in the world." ❧ Kate considered her mom's words. "I think you're right. Meeting Timmy has already made a difference in me. He has a lot of courage. He taught me how to be strong inside and showed me that all kids really just want the same things. They want to be liked and included and they want friends. Now that I know Timmy, I think it's silly I was ever afraid to play with him." ❧ "I'm glad you feel that way, sweetheart," said Kate's mom. "You know, you just

The next morning, Kate bounded down to the breakfast table. She and Timmy had made plans to watch her brother play in a basketball game, but first she needed some answers from her mom. As she filled her cereal bowl, Kate quizzed her mother. ✥ "Mom," Kate said, "why does God make someone like Timmy retarded?" ✥ Her mom stopped what she was doing, sat down at the kitchen table, and looked Kate right in the eye. ✥ "Honey, that's a hard question to answer . . . but what I've come to believe is that God makes us all different. Each of us is here on earth for a reason, and each of us has a special mission to carry out — Timmy included."

Later that night, as Kate lay in bed, she found herself thinking about her new friend, Timmy, and the story her mom had told her. She wondered why God makes life so hard for a kid like Timmy. She wondered, too, about Timmy's mom and dad. How did they feel about having a son like Timmy with a disability? Were they sad? Were they mad? She thought about how hard it must be for Timmy to make friends and to be teased by people who didn't understand he was really a lot like them. As Kate lay there thinking, a tear made its way down her face. She wiped it away, closed her eyes, and went off to sleep.

Together, the two of them headed toward the basketball court. She could hear her friends whispering, but Kate didn't dare turn around to see if anyone was following. She just kept walking forward — her head up and her heart beating faster than it ever had— telling herself over and over to be "strong inside" just as Timmy had said.   When she got to the court, she turned around. One by one her friends walked over to Timmy. Her best friend, Roger, gave him a high five, and then everyone started playing ball. When they finished, they all talked about friends, homework, television, and school. When it was time to go, Timmy and Kate made a play date for the next day.

She was about to continue, but she noticed that all her friends had stopped what they were doing and were just staring at Timmy. No one moved . . . no one spoke. A million thoughts raced through Kate's head. What's wrong with them? Don't they see that they're staring? Can't they tell they're making Timmy feel bad? 🐚 Kate wasn't sure what to do, but she knew she had to think of something fast. She took a deep breath and mustered all her courage. 🐚 "Timmy's my new friend," she announced. "He plays basketball. I asked him to be on my team, and anyone who wants to can come play with us." 🐚 Kate held her breath as she picked up her basketball and handed it to Timmy. 🐚 "Come on, Timmy," she said.

"You are good," Kate said. "Someday we'll play together, okay?" 🕭 Timmy smiled and said, "Thanks, that would be nice . . . really nice." 🕭 Kate nodded and turned to leave, but when she did, she got an idea. She turned quickly back to Timmy and said, "Do you want to play basketball with me and my friends right now?" 🕭 Timmy smiled and said, "I'd like to . . . but do you think they will laugh at me?" 🕭 "No way," said Kate, hoping she was right. 🕭 "What if no one picks me to be on their team?" said Timmy nervously. 🕭 "Don't worry," said Kate. "You'll be on *my* team." 🕭 A huge grin transformed Timmy's face. He looked over at his mom, who nodded yes. Timmy followed Kate to the playground where her friends were playing. 🕭 "Hey, guys," yelled Kate. "This is Timmy. His mom and my mom are friends."

"That's bad," said Kate. "Those kids in your school — they're really rude if they make fun of you for being different." ✆ Timmy shrugged. "Yeah, but I keep going. My mom tells me, 'Be strong inside. Ignore them and keep going. Don't look back.' So that's what I do." Timmy's mom reached for his hand and held it tight. ✆ Kate thought to herself, *Wow! Timmy is strong!* "You know, Timmy," said Kate, "I sometimes have a hard time in school, too. I'm terrible in math. I'm always the last one to finish a test, and I could never finish any of my homework if my mom didn't help me. But I'm good at sports. Do you like sports?" ✆ A big smile crossed Timmy's face, and he shouted, "Yeah, I love basketball. I can dribble really good." ✆ He bounced his ball up and down proudly in front of Kate.

was quiet and shrugged his shoulders. "School's okay, but kids tease me. They call me 'retarded.'" ❧ At that moment Kate could feel her face get red. She tried to think of something to say. She shuffled her feet and looked at the ground. ❧ Then, to her relief, Timmy spoke. "I wish I could learn like other kids, but I have a hard time. I can't do things fast, so kids call me 'slow' and 'dumb.'" ❧ "You mean, they make fun of you in class and stuff?" Kate asked. ❧ "Sometimes they say words like 'dummy' or 'retard' and it makes me sad." ❧ Kate understood what Timmy was talking about. She'd heard kids at her own school call other kids "retard" if they wanted to hurt their feelings. Now that word seemed so mean.

"I like recess, too," said Kate. "It's where I get to play with my friends, and I don't have to do all the hard stuff. Do you play with your friends at recess?" she asked Timmy. ✒ "Sometimes," Timmy said shyly, looking down at the ground. ✒ Then there was a pause and no one said anything. Kate could see that Timmy wasn't as happy as he had been a few minutes before. Oh no, she thought. Did I say something wrong? ✒ Kate's mom noticed her daughter was anxious, so she joined in the conversation. "Well," she said, "I can see you both like the same things about school." Another long pause followed, and Timmy kept looking down. ✒ "Do you like school?" Kate continued. ✒ Timmy

Then Timmy said, "You're the first person to come over and say hi to me. I watch you and your friends play, and you sure run fast." Kate smiled and mumbled, "Thank you." 🐚 For the first time in her life, Kate couldn't think of what to say next. Should she ask a question? What if it was the wrong question? Her mother always had told her there's no such thing as a stupid question, but every question she could think of sounded stupid to her. 🐚 Before she could stop herself, she blurted out, "Do you like math?" She couldn't believe that she'd asked a question about math! She wanted to disappear right then and there. 🐚 "No," Timmy said, shaking his head. "I don't like math. I like recess." 🐚 Kate's and Timmy's mothers both laughed. Then Kate started to laugh. Then Timmy started to laugh, and they all looked at each other laughing.

Kate's mom rose from the park bench and took her daughter's hand. "Let's go meet Timmy. I want you to see for yourself that Timmy isn't someone to be afraid of," she said. Kate felt nervous, but her curiosity was overwhelming, so she agreed. Hand-in-hand, Kate and her mom walked over to where Timmy and his mom were. ❧ "Kate," her mom said, "this is Timmy. Timmy, this is my daughter, Kate. She wanted to meet you. You both are eight years old." ❧ Kate said, "Hi, it's nice to meet you." ❧ "Nice to meet you, too," Timmy repeated. ❧ He spoke very slowly, and Kate had a problem understanding all his words at first. She noticed Timmy's eyes were green like hers and they sparkled when he smiled. He had a big smile like her friend Eduardo and big white teeth like her girlfriend Tanya.

Then Kate looked over again at Timmy. "What's *disabled* mean? Is Timmy disabled? Can he dress himself, eat by himself? Can he go to school?"

⁊ "Wow, Kate! Slow down," her mother urged. "Timmy has what doctors call mental retardation or a developmental disability. His mom just calls him a child with special needs. It means that learning new things like schoolwork or games — or even how to make friends or speak correctly — is harder for Timmy and can take him a lot longer. He needs special help to do math and spelling and . . ." ⁊ "He does *math?*" asked Kate. Kate hated math. Sometimes she cried when she was doing her math homework because she didn't understand it. That was why she couldn't believe Timmy did math, too.

"Grandma explained to me that God makes all different types of children. Some are really athletic, some are artistic. Others have difficulty seeing or hearing. Some do well on tests, some don't. Each of us is unique."   ❧   "What exactly was wrong with Rosie?" Kate asked. "Why was she in a wheelchair?"   ❧   "Grandma told me Rosie was simply a girl who'd had polio, which made it difficult for her to walk. She wasn't someone to feel awkward around."   ❧   Kate wrinkled her forehead. "You mean she was *unabled?*"   ❧   Kate's mother shook her head. "No, the word for someone like Rosie, sweetheart, is physically *disabled.*"

"No, honey, she didn't do anything to me. I was just really surprised . . . kind of shocked . . . when I saw her, because she was in a wheelchair, and I had never seen anyone like that before. You see, in those days we almost never saw anyone like Timmy or Rosie. It was as if people who were different were supposed to stay in their homes or in institutions and not be seen at all." 🐚 Kate's eyes widened. "So what did you do, Mom?" 🐚 "I didn't really know what to do! I just remember feeling funny and staring at her. I'm embarrassed to say I don't think I even spoke to her. I went home that night and told your grandma about Rosie, about how uncomfortable I felt.

"Oh, sure. Let me tell you a story about when I was a little girl growing up back in Maryland. My best friend, Tina, would always come over to *my* house for play dates. She never talked much about her family. All I knew was that her mom and dad both worked a lot, and I knew she had an older sister named Rosie, but that was about it. Then one day, Tina finally invited me to *her* house to play. I was so excited to meet her family." 🐚 "What were they like?" asked Kate. 🐚 "Well, Tina's mom and dad were kind and caring, but her sister, Rosie, was . . . well . . . when I saw her for the first time, I was so uncomfortable and nervous." 🐚 "Why, Mom? What did she do to you? Was she mean? Did she look funny? What? What was it?"

"You see, Kate, Timmy is a child with special needs, and he takes longer to learn than you. He can't walk or run as well as you, and he talks more slowly. But he enjoys and wants all the same things you do. He loves his family, he wants friends, he goes to school, and he dreams about what he wants to be when he grows up . . . just like you. Really, sweetheart, Timmy's a lot like you. That's why it's so important to treat him like any other kid."   "But," Kate persisted, "Timmy's not like anyone in my class. He looks different. He talks funny. I feel weird and scared when I see him."   "Honey, in the beginning we're all uncomfortable with people who may look, talk, or act differently. Even grownups feel that way."   "You mean, you've felt that way too, Mom?"

"When Timmy's mom was pregnant, everyone was so excited. But when he was born, there were a lot of tears." ❧ "Why?" asked Kate. ❧ "Because Timmy was born different from you. The doctor told his parents that their little boy was going to have disabilities and that he wouldn't be able to do all the things you and other kids can do. At first, Timmy's mom was so sad and overwhelmed. She felt like the dreams she'd had for her child would never come true. But as soon as she held Timmy in her arms and looked into his eyes, she fell in love with him just the way he was! She knew right then and there that if she loved him, he'd be the most wonderful child in the world, and that if she worked with him, together they'd build new dreams.

The two women chatted for what seemed like hours. When her mother returned, Kate's words spilled out in a rush.   "Mom," she asked, "who's that boy?"   "That's my friend Anne Potter and her son, Timmy," replied Kate's mother. "Timmy and you were born one month apart in the same hospital. The Potters moved away after you were born and just moved back last week."   Kate couldn't contain herself. "Why does he seem so different? What's wrong with Timmy?"   Kate's mother realized this was a very important question. So she sat her daughter down on the park bench and spoke to her the way she always did when she had something important to say — slowly, clearly, and calmly.

His face seemed flatter than other kids', and he wore glasses that sat crookedly on his face. His foot turned inward, and he walked with a slight limp. When he bounced his ball — as he was doing over and over —

he just didn't do it as well as the other kids she knew. & A pretty woman sat close by on a park bench and joyfully watched the boy. Kate guessed the lady must be his mom because when the boy finished, she clapped and gave him a big hug. & The boy laughed and said proudly in a loud voice, "I can do it, I can do it, Mom!" Then he went back to bouncing his ball. & The boy's excitement fascinated Kate. She grew even more interested when her mother walked over to talk to the boy and his mom.

Once upon a time there was a girl named Kate who was very curious. Curious about everything. Ever since she was little, she'd been asking her mom and dad about everything that interested her — from "How are babies born?" to "What's Heaven?" She wanted the answer to every question, and when she got it, she couldn't wait to share her new knowledge with her friends. ✍ One day Kate and her mom went to the park, where Kate noticed someone she'd never seen before. She couldn't stop staring. She felt funny inside as she looked at a boy standing near her on the playground. He had brown hair like hers, freckles on his nose, and wore a T-shirt and shorts just like her brothers, but he somehow looked different.

Dedication

For my children, Katherine, Christina, Patrick, and Christopher.
May you always reach out to the children who are different
from you with love, compassion, and kindness. To my husband, Arnold, who
shares his life and talents with those with disabilities. Thank you for caring.
To my parents, Eunice and Sargent Shriver,
two extraordinary individuals who have dedicated their lives to
helping those with disabilities. I have seen you change the
world through your determination and love. What a difference you
have made to the millions of people with developmental disabilities.
And, finally, to every parent of a child with special needs,
may we all build new dreams together.

Also by
Maria Shriver

What's Heaven?
Ten Things I Wish I'd Known — Before I
Went Out into the Real World

Acknowledgments

This book would not have been possible without the patience,
wisdom, and assistance of Teri Hess. She helped me with every draft, offered suggestions
over and over, and encouraged me all the way through. I am deeply grateful to her for that
and for her loyalty and support. A big thanks to my fearless agent, Jan Miller, and her
assistant, Shannon Miser-Marven, and to Ellen Jacob, who worked with me on *What's Heaven?*
and now *What's Wrong with Timmy?* Your perceptive eye always lifts my work. Thank you also to
my editors, Maureen Egen, John Keller, and Rick Horgan. They believed in the message of this
book from the start, and I am extremely grateful for their support.

I am forever indebted to my brothers, Timothy and Anthony, who both work every day with the
developmentally disabled. They read and reread every draft of this book and always offered
concrete ways to make it better. I love you both. My thanks also to Billy Kidd, Julia Paige, Erin
Stein, Wanda McDaniel, Anne Sweeney, Andrews Greenleaf, Mike Hardman, Sue Swenson, and
Patricia McGill Smith for their suggestions. And to Jimmy Franco, Beth Mitchell, Sheila
Smallwood, Betty Power, and Linda Jackson for their hard work on this project. Finally, it's an
honor to work with Sandra Speidel, the remarkably talented illustrator of *What's Heaven?* and now
What's Wrong with Timmy? I think we are a great team, and I thank you for believing in this book.

Text copyright © 2001 by Maria Shriver
Illustrations copyright © 2001 by Little, Brown and Company (Inc.) and Warner Books, Inc.

First Edition

Library of Congress Cataloging-in-Publication Data
Shriver, Maria.
What's wrong with Timmy? / by Maria Shriver; Illustrated by Sandra Speidel —1st ed. p. cm.
Summary: Making friends with a mentally retarded boy helps Kate learn that the two of them have
a lot in common.
ISBN 0-316-23337-4
[1. Mentally handicapped— Fiction. 2. Friendship — Fiction.] I. Speidel, Sandra, ill. II. Title.
PZ7.S559173 Wk 2001   [E]—dc21   00-054951
10 9 8 7 6 5 4 3 2 1

Designed by Ellen Jacob and Pegi Goodman

Printed in the United States of America

JP-PLUS
S HR
C. 2

What's Wrong with Timmy?

by Maria Shriver

Illustrated by Sandra Speidel

Warner Books
and
Little, Brown, and Company
AOL Time Warner Companies

Boston   New York   London

P9-DBT-422